LITTLE RABBIT
Goes to Sleep

by Tony Johnston • pictures by Harvey Stevenson

HarperCollins*Publishers*

Library of Congress Cataloging-in-Publication Data
Johnston, Tony.
    Little Rabbit goes to sleep / by Tony Johnston ; pictures by Harvey
Stevenson.
        p.   cm.
    Summary: A little rabbit cannot fall asleep because he finds the night
dark and scary, but when he watches it with his grandfather he sees it
full of stars and crickets and moon.
    ISBN 0-06-021239-X. — ISBN 0-06-021241-1 (lib. bdg.)
    ISBN 0-06-443388-9 (pbk.)
    [1. Fear of the dark—Fiction.   2. Night—Fiction.   3. Bedtime—
Fiction.   4. Grandfathers—Fiction.   5. Rabbits—Fiction.]
I. Stevenson, Harvey, ill.   II. Title.
PZ7.J6478Lj   1994   92-8543
[E]—dc20   CIP
                                                                    AC

For my adored agent,
Susan Cohen,
who never ever sleeps
        —T.J.

For my pal, Suçie
        —H.S.

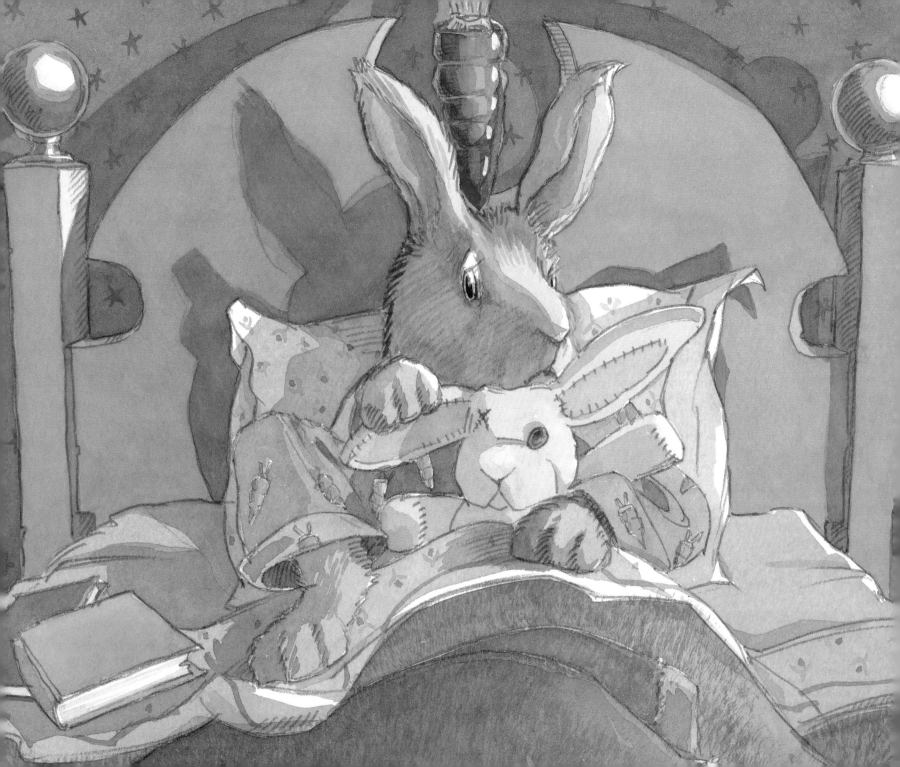

Once a little rabbit could not sleep.
Outside, the night was big and dark,
and he felt very small.

"I will count something
to help me sleep," thought the rabbit.

He heard a mosquito buzzing
somewhere close.
"I will count mosquitoes," he said.
For rabbits do not count sheep.

"One," said the rabbit to the dark.
"One mosquito, all alone."
Still he could not sleep.

He heard little feet
running on the rafters.
Lots of little feet.
Hurrying. Scurrying. Mice feet.

"I will count mice feet
running in the dark."

He listened hard.

He tried hard to count.

But the mice feet hurried too fast
to count a single one.

"Too many feet," he whispered.
And still he could not sleep.

He peeked through the curtains—
just a crack—
to see the darkness.
Something on dark wings
cried out in a nighttime voice
and swooped low.

"Oh," thought the rabbit,
"the night is big and dark
and *scary* too."

So he wriggled down
in his little warm bed
and tried to hide from the scariness.

Under the covers the rabbit heard
creaking in the night.
A nice creaking. A quiet creaking.
It was Grandpa in his rocking chair
on the porch.

So *tiptoe, tiptoe,*
he tiptoed
out of bed and said,
"Grandpa, I cannot sleep.
The night is big and dark."

"Come," said Grandpa. "Come to me.
We will watch the night together."

"Why does night come, Grandpa?"

"So the stars can wink.
Look. They are winking now."

"Why is the night so dark, Grandpa?"

"So the moon can shine
its big silver face at us.
Look."

"Well, I will shine *my* face back at the moon." The rabbit laughed.

He tipped his whiskers to the sky.

He felt he was shining just like the moon.

Then everything was still.

The rabbit whispered, "Grandpa, I hear scary sounds."

"Yes. Very scary." Grandpa laughed.
"Crickets.
This is the song they are singing:

> "*The night is dark.*
>   *The night is still.*
>   *So sing together*
>   *trill-trill-trill.*

> "*The night is black.*
>   *The night is deep.*
>   *So chirp all night*
>   *and never sleep.*"

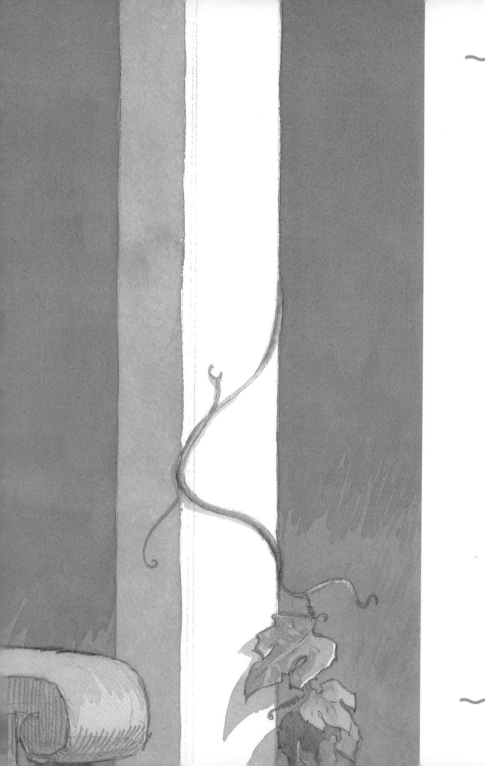

"Can you really hear
what crickets sing?"

"These ears hear
everything."

"I like to watch the night with you,"
the rabbit said.
"It is not scary.
It is full of stars
and crickets and moon."

"This night is full of someone
who should be in bed,"
Grandpa said.

So *tiptoe, tiptoe*, Grandpa took his little rabbit back to bed.

He tucked him in right to his chin.

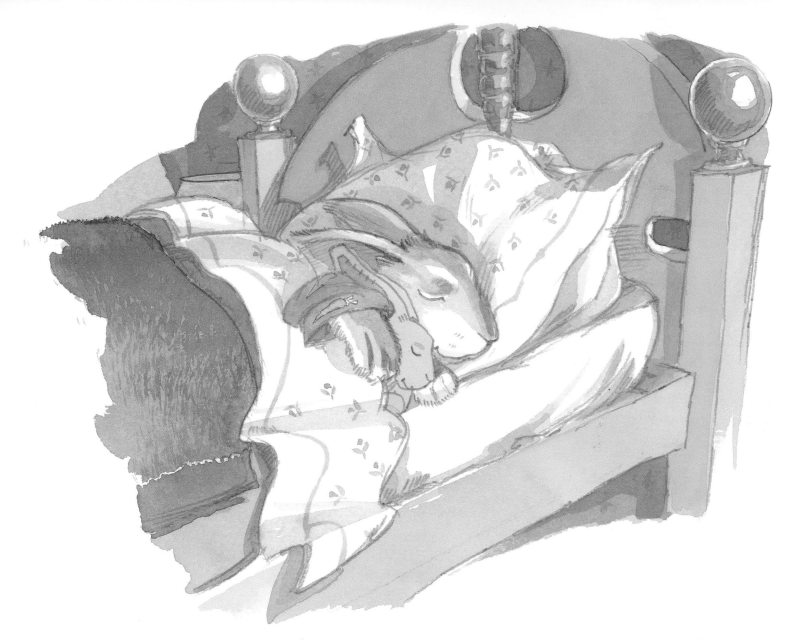

And very soon he slept,
snoring as softly as one little mosquito.

The mice feet were quiet now.
But the crickets still sang
their trilling song.
And the moon stayed silver
all night long.